Crocodile Beat

Written by Gail Jorgensen
Illustrated by Patricia Mullins

Omnibus Books

Down by the river in the heat of the day
the crocodile sleeps and awaits his prey.
Zzzzzzzzz   Zzzzzzzzz   Zzzzzzzzz   Zzzzzzzzz

Ducks are quacking and splashing around.

Quack Quack Quackity

S p l a s h !

Elephants' feet are thumping the ground.

Boom   Boom

Boom-boom-boom!

Monkeys screech and chatter away.
Chitter-chatter Chitter-chatter Chitter-chatter

Eeeeek!

While the birds swoop down to the river to play.

Swish

Swish

Swish

Swish

"Hey," said the lion, "I'm the king.
But I'd be proud to stay and sing."

Rrrrr…oar   *Rrrrr…oar*   *Rrrrr…oar*

R   O   A   R

The bears are clapping and dancing around.
And now they're making their own special sound.

Grrr...owl Grrr...owl Grrr...owl G ROW L

"Wow!" said snake, "What a din!
Sounds like fun — let me join in!"

Hissssss

Hissssss

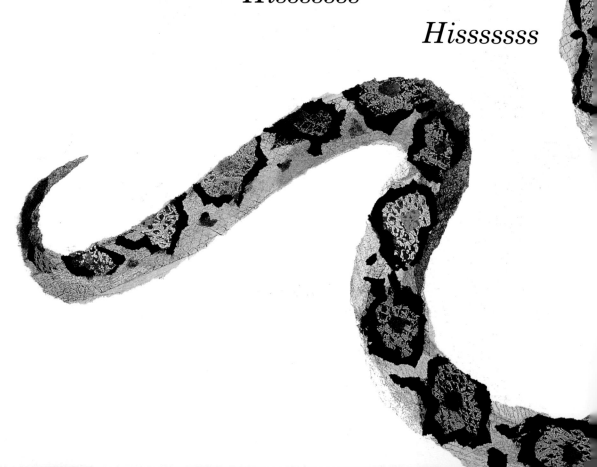

Hissssss

Hisssssss

Ducks and elephants, monkeys, birds,
lion, snake and bears — my word!

Dancing and playing and stomping their feet,
as they move to the rhythm of this jungle beat!

"Ahhhh!" says croc, who wakes with a grin,
"Looks like dinner is here again!"

Watch out animals!
Mean croc's about.
Careful! He'll eat you,
 without a doubt.

Here he comes with a glint in his eye . . .

SNAP!

Oh dear!

Bye-Bye!

Author's Dedication: To Janelle, Kris and Anita, with
thanks also to the children of Elizabeth South Junior Primary School
Illustrator's Dedication: To Hamish

Omnibus Books
A.C.N. 000 614 577
52 Fullarton Road, Norwood, South Australia 5067
part of the SCHOLASTIC AUSTRALIA GROUP
Sydney · Auckland · New York · Toronto · London

First published 1988
First published in paperback 1988
Published in this edition 1997

Typeset by Clinton Ellicott, MoBros, Adelaide
Printed in Hong Kong

National Library of Australia Cataloguing-in-Publication entry
Jorgensen, Gail, 1951–
Crocodile beat.
ISBN 1 86291 319 6.
1. Children's poetry, Australian. 2. Animals—Juvenile poetry.
I. Mullins, Patricia. II. Title. (Series: Bright stars (Norwood, S. Aust.)).
A821.3